DEAD LOCKED

TOM PALMER

With illustrations by
David Shephard

First published in 2015 in Great Britain by
Barrington Stoke Ltd
18 Walker Street, Edinburgh, EH3 7LP

www.barringtonstoke.co.uk

A CIP catalogue record for this book is available from the British Library upon request

ISBN: 978-1-78112-399-7

Printed in China by Leo

For Pauline and Kirsty,
at Leeds Schools Library Service

ONE

When the plane had taken off from Heathrow and the seatbelt signs had gone off, Miss Evans leaned across and handed Owen a book.

"What's this, Miss?" Owen said. He knew the question sounded daft as he asked it.

"A book," Miss Evans said. "For you."

Owen turned it over in his hands and smiled. A present from Miss Evans. That was kind. Really kind. But it was a book.

Deep down inside, Owen had that feeling he always had when books were involved. The churning worry that he wouldn't be able to finish it. But he wouldn't give in to that this time. Miss Evans had given him this, and he could see that it wasn't just any book. It was called *Calon* and the cover was a red Welsh rugby shirt. If there was any book in the world he wanted to read, then this was it.

"Thank you, Miss," Owen said, as the plane dipped to the left and they headed over the clouds towards the Equator and on to New Zealand.

Owen wasn't the only 15-year-old boy on the flight. There was a whole bunch of them, including his two best mates from Borderlands – Woody on his left and Rory on his right. All three were members of the school rugby team, and they were heading to Auckland to take part in the 4-team World Schools Rugby Trophy. Owen couldn't believe it was really happening.

One of the main reasons they were here was sitting in the seat in front of them. Jesse. The team captain. Their star player. Jesse had just signed an under-16 contract with Toulon in France. He was exceptional on the pitch. But he was also an idiot off it. Not someone to get on the wrong side of.

"Tell me again, how many hours will this flight take?" Rory asked Owen.

"Twenty-six altogether," Owen said.

"That's a loooong time," Woody muttered, as he tapped at the video screen on the back of the seat in front of him. He found the BBC News pages and Rory and Owen leaned forward to look.

FIRST FORCES COMING HOME

RAF heads back to UK after conflict in Central Asian Republic

Owen smiled. That was good news for most of his team-mates on this flight. Borderlands was no ordinary school – at least half the pupils had parents in the RAF who'd been involved with the conflict. The RAF had defended the capital city of Lusa and helped its terrified and starving people. One boy who was on the flight – David – had lost his father when a transporter plane was shot down as it delivered aid.

But now the RAF were coming home.

"I'm pleased for you," Owen said to Rory and Woody. "Really pleased."

"Thanks." Rory smiled.

"Yeah, thanks." Woody nodded.

Owen was surprised that his friends didn't sound happier at the news. They were still staring at the screen.

"I thought you'd be happy," Owen said. "Now it's over."

"It's not that easy," Rory admitted, and then he fell silent again.

Then Woody chipped in. "When I know my dad's coming back soon I feel sort of worse than when he's out there," he said. "It's so close. But stuff could still happen ..."

Owen looked at his two friends, trying to understand.

Rory went on. "But the fact they're coming home when we're going away makes it worse too. I seriously thought about not coming so I could see mum and dad home safe."

Owen nodded like he understood. But he didn't, not really. He would never understand what it was like to have a parent in the RAF. He couldn't. Imagine knowing your dad was in a plane and someone was firing surface-to-air missiles at him.

Somewhere over Turkey, Jesse spotted Owen's book.

Owen had been reading it in short bursts, so he could keep focused. But it was late now, after midnight back in the UK. He was sleepy.

"How many pages have you read?" Jesse asked.

"What?" Owen said.

"How. Many. Pages. Have. You. Read?"

Owen knew that this was not a normal friendly question. Jesse didn't do normal friendly questions. He was bored and looking for ways to amuse himself. Maybe he hoped other people were listening so he could show off.

"I'm not sure," Owen said. He stared hard at Jesse.

"Not sure?" Jesse smiled.

"That's right, Jesse."

"Does that mean you can't count – and you can't read?" Jesse mocked. "Bad luck, mate." He held up a super-thin, top-of-the-range Kindle. "Have you got one of these?"

"No," Owen muttered.

"Get with the programme," Jesse sneered. "I've got loads of books on this. I bet I could read them all before you've struggled to the end of chapter 1 of that one."

"Good for you, Jesse." Owen turned away from Jesse and saw that Mr Johnson, head rugby coach at Borderlands, was studying the two of them. Mr Johnson had a look on his face that said 'stop what you're doing'. And he was aiming that look at Jesse.

Jesse went back to his Kindle.

"You OK, Owen?" Mr Johnson asked.

"Yes, sir."

"Good. Try and get some sleep, son."

TWO

"This is awesome," Owen said, as he gazed across the First XV pitch at Auckland Grammar School. "No wonder they're so good at rugby in New Zealand."

Woody and Rory grinned in agreement.

The Borderlands team were on the other side of the world – 12,000 miles from home. Owen felt exhausted and excited at the same time. He was buzzing and completely whacked, just like everyone else. But they had all agreed to stay awake until it was night in New Zealand. And so Auckland School's Head of Sports was showing them around. Players from the host school had joined them too. The different teams hadn't spoken to each other yet, but they'd swapped a few friendly smiles.

The tour took them to the gym, the main hall and three perfect rugby pitches. Before that, wood-panelled corridors lined with trophies and photos of Auckland Grammar School players since 1869. Serious, determined faces of boys from over a hundred years ago. And a roll of honour – a list of the 51 boys who'd gone on to play for the All Blacks. No school in New Zealand had sent more players to the team. What a history! This was some school.

Owen watched Rory kneel and touch the grass, then stare hard at the rugby posts at the end of the pitch.

"This is a perfect surface," Rory said. "Give me a ball. I need to kick one. Now."

Owen and Woody laughed. They'd only been in the country a few hours and already Rory wanted to kick a perfect six from six.

“As long as they don’t start doing the Haka,” Jesse interrupted in a loud voice.

“Will they?” Owen asked, excited. “That would be great. Imagine that before a match. It’d be awesome.”

“Don’t be an idiot,” Jesse said, and his lip curled. “It wouldn’t be fair. It’s cheating. Everyone knows that.”

Owen noticed two of the Auckland boys look over and he felt a hot surge of anger with Jesse. How could anyone say that the Haka was cheating? How embarrassing was that?

Owen also noticed that Mr Johnson was watching. Owen thought that the rugby coach was watching how he reacted to what Jesse had said. It was as if he wanted Owen to sort the argument out. Mr Johnson was like that – he’d give the boys every chance to do the right thing on and off the pitch.

Owen knew what he had to do. He couldn't let the Auckland boys think that all the Borderlands team were as ignorant as their captain. He strode over to the two that had heard Jesse.

"Hi," he said. "I'm Owen. I just want to say we aren't all like him. We don't think that about the Haka. Sorry. He's a ... You know?"

The taller of the two boys grinned. "No worries, mate," he said. "I'm Kane and this is Lucas. And there's idiots in every team. We have our own. Don't worry about it."

Owen smiled.

"What do you think of the pitch then?" Lucas asked. "Not bad, eh?"

"I love it," Owen said.

"When the All Blacks are getting ready for a game in Auckland they train here," Kane said.

"Really?" Owen was thrilled at the idea of playing on the same pitch as the All Blacks. "Do you get to watch?"

Kane nodded. "Yeah. They're our heroes, totally."

"Can I ask ..." Owen said. "I'd like to know ... really, do your school do the Haka before games?"

"Course we do," Kane said.

"Fantastic." Owen grinned. "I hope I get to see it. In the final."

In fact, Owen knew that Borderlands mightn't be playing Auckland at all. Borderlands would begin against the winners of the Australian Schools Trophy, Thomastown. Auckland would then take on Cape Crusaders of South Africa. Both semi-finals would be played on the pitch here at Auckland.

Then the two semi-final winners would play each other. But not here. The final would be held in Eden Park – home of the mighty All Blacks, the New Zealand national team. It was one of the most famous rugby stadiums in the world.

THREE

On the first morning of Borderlands' stay in New Zealand, after a broken night's sleep and a steady training session, Owen and his team-mates went on a tour of Eden Park.

The tour began at the very top of the main stand. Their leader was a tall man in a white shirt, the stadium manager. He introduced himself as Steve, then waited for the boys to settle down.

"So here we are," he announced, "at Eden Park. Home of the All Blacks!"

Owen grinned. The view was amazing. A huge pitch. Four stands. Tens of thousands of seats facing into one of the world's great theatres of sport. Beyond it was the city of Auckland with the point of the Sky Tower reaching into the blue and a range of mountains in the background.

Owen could tell that Steve was very proud of his stadium. And who could blame him? But Owen could also see that at least three of his team-mates were looking at their phones – and not paying any attention.

"It's brilliant," Owen said. He wanted to show Steve that he – at least – was impressed by Eden Park. He was embarrassed that his team-mates seemed more interested in their phones. Jesse was doing it. Even Rory! He couldn't believe it.

Owen made his way towards Rory. "What are you doing?" he hissed. "We should be listening to the tour."

"They're back," Rory said.

"What?"

"The squadron. They're back home."

Now Owen understood. He felt himself cringe, ashamed to have challenged Rory like that. Their parents were home from the war. Texts were flooding in from home. There wasn't a building in the world that would impress them right now.

A little later, at the next stage of the tour, the Borderlands team were joined by another group of boys. Thomastown School from Sydney, Australia.

"And this," Steve said, "is the tunnel. One of you teams will walk down it and out onto the pitch when you play in the final in a week's time. Out of the dressing room used by the likes of Richie McCaw and Jonah Lomu."

"You Poms had best have a good look round now," one of the Australian players joked. "You'll not be here on Friday."

"We will be here," Jesse snapped.

"No way. This is too big a stage for you boys," another of the Australians said. "You're in the southern hemisphere now. Where the English come to lose."

Owen smiled. Aussie sledging. It always got under the skin of English players. At times like this, he felt extra proud to be Welsh.

"Like 2003?" Jesse snapped again. He stood in front of the two Australian boys, so they had to stop or collide with him. "That was at your place, wasn't it? The World Cup Final, I seem to remember?"

"Ancient history, mate. I'm talking about this week." The Australian boy was smiling. He had Jesse totally out-classed.

Then Steve led both teams into a supply tunnel that ran underneath the stadium and into the home dressing room. The argument rumbled on. Owen watched Jesse carefully. He was fuming – the Australians had got to him big time. Owen just hoped that it wouldn't make Jesse mess up his game tomorrow.

FOUR

The whole Borderlands team were staying in the Auckland Grammar School boarding house, a big white wooden building that overlooked the rugby pitches. They had five dorms with four boys in each.

Owen woke the next morning long before Woody and Rory. The time difference between home and New Zealand was bothering him. His body felt sluggish and heavy, and his mind had no idea whether it was day or night. He'd been wide awake since 3 a.m. He'd passed the time reading *Calon*, the book Miss Evans had given him, then closing his eyes and kidding himself he was asleep.

Owen wanted to give the book everything he could. He knew he had to keep the momentum going if he was going to finish it, and so he was reading it in short bursts every time he got a chance. Which wasn't a problem – he was loving it. It was thrilling to find out about George North, the Millennium Stadium and how the Welsh team trained. More than that, Owen felt like he was there with them, that he was one of them.

The title of the book – *Calon* – meant "heart" in Welsh. And it made Owen's heart swell just to look at the photos, the red shirts and white shorts. Now he understood why the New Zealand boys filled their school with photos of their incredible rugby heritage.

As he drifted off again, Owen was disturbed by the sound of something outside. Footsteps. He perched on the end of his bed and stared out between the curtains. It was barely light outside. But he could make out shadows, the shapes of people walking down towards the school. Boys wearing shorts and rugby boots, carrying towels.

They were training!

Owen checked the time. 6.15 a.m. He had to admire their dedication.

Borderlands never trained as a team before the school day started. Rory was known to sneak out at all hours with his notebook and ball to work on his kicking, but no one else would start so early.

Owen leaned out of the window to watch the squad do laps of the rugby pitches, then a series of stretches. When they finished, half an hour had gone and the sun was up.

Owen looked back into his room and saw that only one other bed had someone in it – Thomas's. So where were Woody and Rory? Owen hadn't noticed them get up.

Owen slipped out of bed and opened the door to the common area between all the boys' rooms. There were giant beanbags in one corner and a huge TV screen decorated with New Zealand rugby flags with their famous silver fern. Woody and Rory were leaning over a pool table at the other end of the room. They were both staring at Woody's iPad, which was propped up on the green felt of the table.

"What's up?" Owen whispered.

Rory looked round. "Woody's trying to Skype his dad. I've tried my mum and dad. It's 8 p.m. at home. We thought ..." Rory stopped.

"No joy?" Owen asked. He could see that his friend was upset.

"No. I can't get it to connect. But it should work. I've done everything like you're meant to."

"I'm sorry," Owen said. "Maybe it's just the Wi-Fi in here."

"It's everything," Woody said. "We've not had any texts either. Just some information would be good."

"I just want to see them in the front room at home," Rory said. "You know?"

Owen nodded. But, like the stuff they'd talked about on the flight, he didn't know. And he wasn't sure what to do to help his friends.

"Erm ... do you want a cup of tea?" he asked.

And then Rory and Woody were laughing out loud. So loud Owen was worried they'd wake the other boys up.

Owen went red. "What?" he asked. "What did I say?"

Once they had stopped laughing, Woody explained. "That's what people always do. Make a cup of tea. Nine times out of ten you can't contact your parents. And there's always someone there to make a cup of tea. Yes, Owen, I'd love one. Thank you."

"Me too." Rory grinned.

Owen smiled, too. At least he knew he wasn't any more useless than anyone else. He would make them some tea. That's what you did.

"Earl Grey," Woody said, as Owen walked towards the kitchen.

"What?" Owen was puzzled.

"Do you have Earl Grey? Or Lapsang do-dah?"

"Ermmmm." Owen wasn't sure what to say.

Rory started laughing again. Then Woody.

Owen nodded and grimaced. "I'll just take a flight to Lapsang. Get you some of that fancy tea and bring it back. Won't be long."

FIVE

That afternoon, Owen stood with his Borderlands team-mates on the main pitch at Auckland. To his right was their amazing club house. To his left, the players from the Australian team were warming up. Some of the boys were talking to Jesse across the halfway line.

This was it.

The semi-final of the World Schools Rugby Trophy.

Borderlands against Thomastown of Australia.

Owen breathed in and out to calm himself down.

Then he looked at his two best friends to see how they were coping. Rory was standing with his back to the team, staring into space. Woody was too. Owen knew that wasn't right. Not right at all. In fact, the whole feel of the team wasn't right for the start of a match. Everyone was in their own world.

'They're worrying about their parents,' Owen thought. 'And why shouldn't they? Their parents are way more important than rugby.'

But the fact remained that this was rugby. It was really important rugby. They all had to give it 100% or they might as well not have bothered flying all the way round the world to play in the tournament.

Owen looked for Jesse. He was the one who should be doing something now. He was their captain – he should be giving everyone a boost, bringing them together. He needed to make them forget their families for a couple of hours and focus on the game instead. But Owen could see that Jesse was too busy sledging the Australians. And Mr Johnson had already done his team talk in the dressing room.

So Owen decided that he should do something. He was one of the few who didn't have to worry about his mum and dad.

"Lads," he called out. "Lads!"

Only Rory and Woody looked round. No one else.

Owen decided to go for it. He shouted this time. "Lads! Gather round."

And they did. One by one, then in twos and threes, the whole Borderlands team came to stand in a semi-circle around Owen. Only Jesse and David ignored him. They were still right up on the halfway line, chest to chest with the opposition.

Owen breathed in again. He decided to ignore Jesse and David. He had to talk to the team.

"I can't imagine what it's like having your mum or dad away at war," he said to them all. "I can't imagine what it's like to have them come back when you're not there, when you're on the other side of the world." Owen paused. "But I can imagine it must feel rubbish. So can I say something?"

Four lads said yes. None said no. Owen took it as permission.

"I was with you at Twickenham when we won the National Schools Trophy. I was with you when we won in Toulon. We're the European champions. And we won both those finals when your parents were fighting a war." Owen paused for a second. "I don't know how you did that. I'm amazed by what you can do."

Owen saw that the semi-circle of boys was moving into a huddle. Arms were going round shoulders. There was a grittier look in his team-mates' eyes. They were starting to behave more like they were a rugby team before a big game.

"If you could do that then," Owen went on, "I think you can do it again today. You know your parents are home or are coming home. You wish you were there too. But you're here. And, like I said, I can't imagine it, but I know you all and I think you can do it again today."

Owen stopped. He wondered if he sounded like a fool, making this big fancy speech. But he saw that all eyes were on him. There was that gritty look of determination in those eyes. Perhaps his speech had worked.

And then – as they broke up the huddle – there was a rush of noise. The doors of Auckland Grammar School were flung open. All of a sudden, the walkways were filled with

hundreds of boys pouring out of the school. The whole school stampeded down to watch the game. They filed round all sides of the pitch, and most of them massed on the concrete steps to Owen's right. The noise of their feet and their shouts was thrilling. Owen felt it and he could see all his team-mates were feeling it too. Everything had changed. The mood had gone from downcast to upbeat.

Jesse ambled over to the team huddle just as it broke up. "Are we ready, lads?" he asked.

"We're ready," Owen said.

"Ready to hammer these Australians?" Jesse grinned.

After the match, Owen reflected that two things had made the difference – had made it a remarkable game.

First, every single one of the New Zealanders were supporting Borderlands.

"I reckon they want the Aussies to lose," Woody said to Owen during a break in play. "More than wanting us to win."

"I reckon you're right."

The second thing, Owen had to admit, was Jesse.

He was a machine. He killed them.

From the very start he played the right passes to the right players at the right time. He made the right calls, spotted all the right weaknesses in the Thomastown line. Every time.

As the game went on, Owen could see that his team-mates had thrown off their tension and worries and were going for it. They were matching Jesse with the quality and precision of their play.

By half-time the score was 21–7.

By full-time, it was 49–19.

Jesse was on fire. The match let him show all his brilliance as a rugby player.

But as soon as the game was over, they all saw the bad side of Jesse. Owen watched him march over to his opposing number.

"How was that?" Jesse asked, right in the Aussie boy's face. "How the hell was that? How about you come and watch us at Eden Park in the final? I'll get you a ticket if you like."

The Australian captain was having none of it. He put his hands square on Jesse's chest and pushed him away, hard. But Jesse had a mad look in his eyes. He was wired. So Owen made a decision. He ran over and grabbed Jesse round the chest, then pulled him back. Just before fists were about to fly.

Owen fell, Jesse on top of him, still lashing out with fists and feet.

Then Mr Johnson was there. And the referee.

The fight was over before it started.

And Borderlands were in the final of the World Schools Rugby Trophy.

SIX

"We're in the final."

"We beat the Aussies."

"We're playing at Eden Park."

The mood of the Borderlands team after the match was amazing. There were tables laid out with a post-match meal, but they were all too excited to sit and eat.

Borderlands were in the club house that overlooked the rugby pitches, so that they could watch the second semi-final as guests of the home school. At one end there were huge windows looking out on the pitch. At the other was a wooden panel, which listed the names of the 51 All Blacks who had attended the school, and a framed All Blacks shirt. This place was beyond serious about rugby. There was no doubt in Owen's mind about that now.

The second semi-final was Auckland School versus Cape Crusaders of South Africa. The winners would play Borderlands in the final.

"You did well, lads," Mr Johnson said, as he came into the club house. "Very well, in fact. I didn't expect us to turn them over so completely. But you did it. All credit to you. Whoever wins this match will be wary of us in the final now."

"We'll destroy them," Jesse boasted, as the Kiwi and South African teams walked onto the pitch and lined up facing each other.

"I doubt that, Jesse," Mr Johnson said. "They're both great teams. Do you realise what it takes to be the best school rugby team in New Zealand or South Africa? Something very special, that's what. Something you've never come up against before. So we need to watch their every move. Like they've watched ours. They know our strengths and weaknesses. They'll be analysing those. Now we have to find out theirs."

Mr Johnson stopped and the boys all looked out of the club-house windows.

Woody nudged Owen. "Look, Auckland are going to do the Haka."

Owen watched as the Auckland boys lined up, ten metres shy of the halfway line.

"Fantastic," Owen said. "I've never seen this apart from on TV."

And the Haka began.

All 15 Auckland Grammar School boys were wearing black shorts and blue shirts so dark they looked black. Owen noticed Kane pacing among them, starting their Haka. He looked different to the easy-going boy Owen had spoken to the day before. He started the chant alone, pacing between two lines of his team-mates. Then, suddenly, the whole team let out a chant. Owen felt a shiver go down his spine. Then the Auckland team squatted to put their fists to the ground, stuck their tongues out and fell to their knees. All the time they chanted in deep voices that Owen could feel vibrating in his chest, even from the side of the pitch.

Owen felt emotion and excitement course through him just watching it. He wanted Auckland to win so he could stand with the Borderlands squad and face those boys as they did the Haka at Eden Park. How could he go home and not have had that experience?

Then Jesse broke into Owen's trance. "I don't get why the South Africans just let them do it," he said. "When they do the Haka to us, we'll have an answer for it."

‘Typical Jesse,’ Owen thought. He could never let anything go without some nasty remark. The captain’s bad attitude was starting to grate on Owen’s nerves.

“Good idea. What did you have in mind?” an adult voice said.

Owen had to look twice to see who it was.

Mr Searle.

Owen couldn’t believe that their assistant coach was agreeing with Jesse that he should disrupt the Haka.

And nor did Mr Johnson.

“That is not happening,” the head coach said in a sharp voice. “Do you understand me, Jesse? And, Mr Searle, please don’t encourage the boys to be so disrespectful.”

The mood in the club house shifted. It was a warm day, but there was a definite chill in the air now.

"Understood?" Mr Johnson repeated. He glared at Jesse before he walked over to speak to the coach of the Auckland team, who had just come into the club house. The two men walked out of the room.

Jesse didn't acknowledge Mr Johnson's glare. The minute the head coach had gone, he stood up and kicked a chair out of the way.

He looked angry, really angry.

"You don't have to do anything, sir," Jesse said to Mr Searle. "But when they do the Haka at us we're going to walk right through them. Like the French did in the World Cup Final." Then he raised his voice. "There is no way we're going to sit back and take that."

Owen cringed. He wanted to see the Haka. He wanted to admire it, not be scared of it. Jesse was threatened by its power. That much was clear. But how many people get to face the Haka before a game? Owen was sure that it would make him play harder. Some of the ideas he'd read about in *Calon* came to mind. That you should be proud of the team you play for. You should give the game everything. But – above all – you should respect the opposition. Without that respect, you'd lose and, more than that, respect was the right attitude – the only attitude.

"I'm with you, Jesse," Mr Searle said. "I've always thought the Haka was a disgrace."

"I'm a Toulon player after the final," Jesse said. "I'm leaving the school. And if Johnson wants to win the World Cup for Borderlands he needs me in the team. He can stick it. Without me ..."

"Jesse. Outside now." Mr Johnson was back, and he was standing over them. His bulk seemed even bigger, casting a dark shadow.

Jesse had been too caught up in his own anger to notice Mr Johnson coming back.

"You too, Mr Searle," Mr Johnson said.

Owen watched Mr Johnson march to the exit. Mr Searle and Jesse had no choice but to follow in his wake.

SEVEN

The Borderlands team tried to focus on watching the second semi-final. But they knew something massive was going on in the next room. They could all hear Mr Johnson's voice coming through the wall. He wasn't shouting, but his voice was so deep that it still carried.

Miss Evans came to sit next to Owen.

"Well played today, Owen," she said. "You'll have the Welsh Rugby Union after you if you carry on like that."

"Thanks, Miss."

"How's the book?"

"Good, Miss," Owen said. "I'm nearly on page 100."

Miss Evans clapped her hands as if someone had scored a try. "Brilliant! 100 pages. You used to struggle to reach page 10 in any book. Now look at you."

Owen blushed. It did feel good. He was doing well and he knew it.

"It's a great book, Miss," Owen said. "Thanks."

On the pitch, six minutes in, Auckland Grammar School scored a try.

Off the pitch, Owen heard a loud noise. A door slamming or a chair being kicked over. Again.

Then all the boys watched as Jesse and Mr Searle appeared outside the club house. They both walked away, through the car park and up towards the boarding house.

“What’s going on?” Woody asked Owen. “Looks pretty dramatic from here.”

Owen shrugged.

“I just hope he doesn’t drop him,” Andrew said.

“We’ve no chance if he does,” George agreed.

“He’d never do that,” Gareth said. “He’ll warn him or fine him. You don’t drop your best player, even if he is a ... you know.”

Then the door opened and Mr Johnson appeared. His face was red with rage.

“Boys. Can I have a brief word, please?”

All eyes were on the head coach. No one was watching the other semi-final now.

“You all witnessed what went on there, I know,” Mr Johnson said.

"Yes, sir," several of the boys said.

"And you also know that I gave Jesse a final warning about his conduct when we were at the European finals in Toulon."

Now no one spoke. They didn't want to take in the logic behind what Mr Johnson was saying. But Owen knew what was coming. Jesse had his final warning in France. And now this further outrage had happened here.

"I've told Jesse and Mr Searle to pack their bags," Mr Johnson said. "They'll travel home on the next flight we can arrange for them. They'll not be staying at the boarding house with the rest of us."

"Home, sir?" asked David – Jesse's only friend on the team.

"Yes," Mr Johnson said. "Home. To Borderlands. They're off the tour. I'm sorry to do this to all of you. I know how excited you are about this tournament, and all the work you've put in. But in school and in rugby there must be discipline. Above all else. Thanks to Jesse's actions, you need to think about who your next captain will be."

"Yes, sir," the boys said.

Mr Johnson began to walk away. Then he stopped and turned.

"Look, boys ..." His tone of voice had dropped. "You will have questions. You may want to challenge me on this. But I've made my decision. I'm too angry to talk about it now and I need to watch Auckland play Cape Crusaders to see what we're going to be up against in the final. So do you. But if you want to come and talk to me about it, perhaps later this evening, I'd be open to that. Until then, enjoy the rest of the game and please don't speak to anyone else about our troubles."

With a last glance around, his face more sad than angry now, Mr Johnson left the room.

For the rest of the first half none of the boys spoke. They were all staring at the pitch. But Owen knew that they were all thinking about how they felt about Jesse being sent home. And Mr Searle too. Some of them might be angry with Mr Johnson for being so harsh. Others might be pleased to see the back of their captain. All of them would be upset in one way or another.

Then at half-time – when the score was 34–0 to Auckland – David stood up.

"We've got problems," he said.

Two or three of the boys laughed. But they were dry, nervy laughs.

"The first problem," David said, "is that we need a captain."

"How about you?" Andrew, the Borderlands hooker, said.

"No." David shook his head. "I'm not a captain."

"What's the second problem?" Gareth asked.

David frowned. "That, at this rate, we're going to lose the final."

Owen smiled. He liked David sometimes. And he was right about both things. The team had two huge problems that they needed to sort out. And fast.

EIGHT

The Borderlands boys met in the boarding house by the pool tables. They sprawled in a circle on giant bean bags. But no one was relaxed – they had a decision to make.

Owen had no idea who his team-mates would choose as captain. He didn't even know who he would vote for himself. Jesse had always been captain. He was an idiot, yes – but he had a very strong personality. So strong they'd never considered anyone else as captain.

Again it was David who spoke first. "Does anyone have anything to say?" he asked.

No one spoke.

"Anyone got anything to say about what happened to Jesse?" he repeated.

The question hung in the air. Owen wondered if people were too worried to say what they thought, since they knew that David was Jesse's friend. They might be scared to say that they were sick of Jesse being an idiot.

So Owen raised his hand. If they were going to sort this out, someone had to be honest and it might as well be him.

"Owen?" David said.

"I think Mr Johnson did the right thing," Owen said. "Jesse went too far. Again and again. Mr Johnson warned him, but he wouldn't stop. Mr Johnson had to punish him in the end."

"But we've got no chance in the final now," George complained. "We'll lose."

"Jesse's not our only player," Owen said. "Rory scores most of our points. We just have to play to our strengths. Get penalties."

Owen saw Rory looking straight at him. Determination was etched into his face. Owen knew he'd said the right thing.

"Good point," David said. "But we do need a new captain."

"And scrum half," Andrew said. "A decent one."

"To be honest, I'd have chosen you to be captain," Owen said to David. "But you've said you don't want it."

"I don't."

"Who votes for David?" George broke in.

Five hands went straight up. But no more.

David smiled. "See? Five? That's not enough. I'm not right for some of you. I'm not the one to be your leader."

No one spoke. They all knew he was right.

"But I can tell you who I think should be captain. And scrum half," David said. "And I bet at least ten of the hands in the room go up when I say his name."

"Who?" Gareth asked.

"Owen."

Owen stared at David in amazement. Had David really said that? Was he joking? Owen felt OK about being scrum half. He'd played scrum half for the Second XV, before he made the Firsts. But captain?

"Remember when we were in France and Jesse was being so ... stupid?" David said. "Remember how the team vibe was rock bottom? Who changed that?"

"Owen," Andrew said.

"And remember at the start of this week, when everyone was feeling low just before the semi kicked off and Jesse and I were squabbling with the Aussies? Who motivated the team then?"

"Owen," three or four voices said.

Owen noticed hands going up around the room. His eyes went from team-mate to team-mate. Woody. Rory. Rhys. Thomas. And David's hand was up now too.

"And who just said he thought we could win the final? Who's the first person to make us feel like we could do it since Jesse got himself chucked off the team?"

All hands in the room were up now.

"Well, then," David said. "There's our decision."

Owen's instinct was to say no. But he knew that if he did – and it looked like no one else was up for doing it either – then Borderlands would lose the final. He realised that he needed time to think it over.

"I have to sleep on it," Owen said. "Can I tell you in the morning? Please?"

"Sure," David said.

Owen stood up. He felt embarrassed. Everyone was looking at him.

"Right then," he said. "I'd better go to bed."

A couple of the team laughed. At least there was a better feeling in the room now.

"I'll think about it," Owen went on, as he backed towards his bedroom door. "Tell you tomorrow."

This time, all his team-mates laughed.

"Sweet dreams."

"Don't let the bed bugs bite."

Owen grinned as he closed the door of the room he shared with Rory, Woody and Thomas. His mind was all over the place. There was no chance he could think clearly about being captain. But he had to. Did he have what it took to captain a rugby team in a World Cup final?

He felt his breathing go shallow and his heart pick up a beat. He needed to calm himself down.

Then Owen saw his book. *Calon.*

He'd read that. Then sleep. He could make his mind up in the morning.

NINE

Owen climbed into bed and reached for *Calon*. He took out the card that he was using as a bookmark and looked at it. It was a note from Miss Evans.

Enjoy. Be inspired. Cael y Calon.

Half an hour later he was still reading. About Wales winning the Grand Slam. About Sam Warburton, the Wales captain. About what it took to be a world-class rugby player.

Then, before he knew it, it was morning. Light was coming in through the curtains. Outside he could hear the strange high-pitched whooping sounds of a bird he'd never heard before. And his face was pressed on a hard surface.

Owen looked down to see what he'd been sleeping on.

His book.

It was all he could do not to laugh.

It was still half dark in the bedroom, so Owen got dressed and went out, in the hope he wouldn't wake the others.

Outside he laughed a proper laugh. Something huge had happened.

He'd fallen asleep reading his book.

Owen had never fallen asleep reading a book before. He could feel his heart beating faster just at the thought of it. He'd not given up, got bored, found it too hard, or stopped because his mind couldn't go on working out all the words. He'd stopped because he had fallen asleep. But he could remember every word he'd read as he tried to keep his eyes open. About the Grand Slam win. The stadium, the players, the pace and energy of each game. It was all so vivid that he'd felt like he was there with the Welsh players. He found it hard to believe a book could make him feel that way.

Owen looked at his watch. It was six in the morning. He was suddenly really hungry, so he wandered into the dining room of the boarding house. He assumed he would be the first one there.

But he wasn't. Miss Evans was already there.

"Hello, Owen," she said.

"Hi, Miss."

"Can't sleep?" she asked.

"No," Owen said. "But I've got something to tell you."

"What's that?"

"The book you gave me. *Calon.* I love it. It's giving me a real lift. I reckon I should take it on the pitch with me at the final. It's that good, Miss."

As Owen and Miss Evans ate, the Auckland students started to file in and sit at their regular tables. None of the other Borderlands players were up yet.

"Miss?" Owen said.

"Yes, Owen."

"They've asked me to be captain."

"Who has?" Miss Evans asked.

"The team. All of them."

Miss Evans put down her coffee cup. "And?"

Owen hesitated. He'd wanted to talk to Miss Evans because he thought she could help persuade him to do it.

But that was a mistake.

Now that he'd opened his mouth, he realised that he felt so good and so strong about reading *Calon* that he felt good and strong about himself in every way.

It was a weird feeling, but the book had given him heart.

Just like Miss Evans had written in her card.

Just like the title of the book.

"I'm going to say yes," Owen told Miss Evans. "I'm going to captain Borderlands in the final."

TEN

That morning the Borderlands team played at being tourists. Mr Johnson had arranged a day trip to the New Zealand National Museum of Rugby. A bus came for them after breakfast.

Before the bus set off, Owen told the others that he would be happy to be their captain.

The three cheers that followed made him blush.

But he made sure he looked each of them in the eye. In *Calon* he'd read that's what Sam Warburton did in the huddle before matches. If he was going to be like any captain, he'd be like him.

The bus took them to the airport.

They travelled from Auckland to Palmerston North in a small plane that flew low enough for Owen to see every inch of the rugged landscape of New Zealand. The pilot told them about the extinct volcanoes they were travelling over and how a huge fault in the earth's structure ran through a cross section of the country, which is what made the New Zealand landscape so remarkable. He pointed out lands that belonged to the Maori people and he spoke about the country's history before Europeans arrived. He even explained about the Haka and how it was a war dance used by the Maoris to prepare themselves for battle.

Owen loved hearing about New Zealand. The pilot brought his country to life and Owen was really looking forward to the rugby museum by the time they landed 40 minutes later.

The museum wasn't big. There was a set of display cases around a netted area where some of the boys took part in kicking and scrum challenges. The displays were full of balls and shirts and images showing 150 years of rugby in New Zealand.

Owen was drawn like a magnet to the Haka display. He was worried that his interest in the New Zealand pre-match ritual was becoming an obsession. But he couldn't help himself.

He read that the Haka had first been done by a warrior chief who was fleeing his enemies. When he'd turned and performed a Haka, they had all run away. But it wasn't the story that did it for Owen. It was listening to the Haka that sent a shiver down his spine, as he faced the large photo of the All Blacks delivering it. It was like nothing he'd ever heard. Not like poetry. Not like music. Not like shouting or singing. It was unique.

Mr Johnson was standing behind Owen. "How does it make you feel?" he asked.

"Excited," Owen admitted. "I like it. I know I'm meant to be intimidated, but ..."

"No." Mr Johnson shook his head. "You've got the right attitude. The Haka is a war dance. The Maoris did it before they went into battle. To fire themselves up. To warm up. They use every muscle they have when they do it. To prepare to fight. You can take it two ways. You can be afraid of it. Or you can be inspired by it."

"I'm inspired, sir," Owen said. "Definitely."

"Good." Mr Johnson lowered his voice. "Because I think Jesse was intimidated by it."

Owen said nothing.

"I'm pleased they chose you, Owen," Mr Johnson said at last. "And I'm pleased you accepted. Miss Evans told me about your chat this morning."

"Yes, sir."

"You've done well. I'm proud of you."

"Thank you, sir."

There was another pause. Then Mr Johnson lowered his voice for a second time. "I want you to know that I would have chosen you too, Owen," he said.

Owen looked at his rugby master. "Really, sir?"

"Really, Owen. I think you've already proved you'll be a great captain. I'll ask you to speak to the boys about the Haka before the final, if I may?"

"You may, sir," Owen said with a grin.

*

After the museum, the boys had an hour to explore Palmerston North. Most of them hung around a large park by a square of shops, with a war memorial at its centre.

Owen noticed that Woody, Rory and some of the others were in a café on the edge of the park. They sat outside, with their iPads and their phones out.

Owen knew they were trying to contact home. But he also knew that they had no chance. It was 4 a.m. back home. His team-mates must be desperate if they were trying now.

And when he saw them shuffle from the café to the bus he could see how dejected they were.

Not good. Dejection was not what he wanted his team to be feeling.

As captain he'd have to do something to lift their spirits. Or Borderlands would have no chance of performing at their best in the final of the World Schools Trophy, let alone winning it.

ELEVEN

Two days later, the bus carrying the Borderlands players drew up at Eden Park. It went in a large iron gate and under the main stand, then it passed into the service tunnel. Owen gazed at the stands and turf and Eden Park signs. He couldn't quite believe they were going to play here.

All the players were aware that Mr Johnson was watching them from the front of the bus.

"This is how teams like Australia and England and Wales arrive here for a match," he said. "So you deserve to come in the same way."

They came to a halt and Owen led his team off the bus. As he did, he noticed that everyone stole a glance out along the tunnel at the green of the pitch, before they turned towards the dressing rooms. These were the same dressing rooms they had seen on the tour. Except, this time, there were 15 yellow and blue Borderlands shirts where the shirts of Richie McCaw and Jonah Lomu had hung.

"Let the lads settle in first," Mr Johnson said in a low voice to Owen as they went into the dressing room. "Then I'll do my team talk. And you say a few words too. OK?"

"OK," Owen said. Then he watched his team-mates, judging their mood. Some were trying out the warm-up bikes at the far end of the dressing room, loosening their muscles. Others were using the loos.

"I just peed where Dan Carter peed," Rahim said.

"How do you know?" Danny asked. "He might not have used the one you did."

"I peed in all three," Rahim replied.

Owen smiled as several of the Borderlands team laughed. He was pleased. There was a good relaxed feel among them. If they were going to stand any chance in this match, they needed to be relaxed. It was the final of the World Schools Rugby Trophy. There was no bigger game than this for a schoolboy.

Just before Borderlands were due to go out, Mr Johnson called the team together.

"I'll keep this short, lads," he said. "We've already talked tactics. We've studied their play, decided on a plan. You're about to play in the final of the World Schools Trophy. At Eden Park. This is, without doubt, the biggest game of your lives so far."

The coach paused so the players could take in his words.

"You will be nervous," Mr Johnson went on. "And you should be nervous. I want you to be nervous. But you're relaxed too, settled in yourselves. I overheard Rahim joking just now. A magic moment, no doubt." There was laughter in his voice. "But one day Dan Carter was here in this dressing room on his debut for the All Blacks. He will have been nervous that day too."

Mr Johnson smiled.

"But you can be sure that once he was on the pitch, he will have done what every player must do when they play here. He will have given it everything. You can be nervous, relaxed, laughing, feeling sick. You can be all those things and more, and you can – and must – give it everything on the pitch. I believe in you, in Borderlands. And I know that you'll give it your all."

Mr Johnson stepped to one side and waved for Owen to stand up.

"We all know there was trouble about Jesse and the Haka," the coach added. "His attitude was wrong. But I think your captain has it right. So I'd like to ask Owen to prepare us for the Haka. Owen?"

This was it.

Owen tried to smile, but his face didn't quite work. He knew he was their captain, but it was hard to take it in when someone called him that.

He struggled to level out the shake in his voice. "I just wanted to say ..." he said, then started again. "I just wanted to say that when we were at the museum a few days ago, I spent a lot of time staring at that Haka display. Who else saw it?"

Owen watched as every player's hand went up. He saw their faces as one. They looked serious. They were listening.

"When I looked at that display I was afraid I'd be nervous facing the Haka today," Owen said. "But then I felt something else. The Haka is about to be performed to us – at Eden Park. There is nothing about the Haka we need to worry about."

Owen could sense that he was beginning to speak faster.

"And that's because we've earned the right to face down the Haka," he went on. "We're one of the two best school rugby teams on the planet. It's our right to face the Haka. It's our right to draw power and energy from it. And it's our right to be playing in the World Schools final. Am I right? Am I right?"

The roar that went up was so loud that Owen was sure the Auckland boys would have heard it in their dressing room.

'Good,' he thought. 'That's no bad thing.'

TWELVE

The noise of the roar from the Borderlands team was nothing compared to the noise of the crowd. Owen was the first to see why it was so loud. The two stands running the length of the pitch were as good as full. There had to be 30,000 people watching.

Owen could see that some of his team-mates were shocked by the noise and size of the crowd.

"Let's focus, lads," he shouted. "Line up. Face the home team."

He wanted them to forget about the crowd as soon as they could.

In their dark blue shirts and black shorts, the New Zealand champions could have been mistaken for the All Blacks themselves. They stood strong against the black letters spelling out 'EDEN PARK' on the stand behind them.

Owen had said everything he needed to say about the Haka. He just hoped it would give his team-mates strength, not the opposite.

Then it began. Kane from Auckland walked up and down among his team-mates, whipping them into a frenzy. The sounds of the Maori language filled the stadium, echoing from stand to stand.

To Owen it was amazing to watch their faces, their staring eyes, their posture as they performed their dance. He could feel a real surge of power coming from the Kiwi boys. But it wasn't a power that was working against him and his team. It was a power that seemed to fill the stadium, pouring into both teams and the huge crowd too. The roar they gave up at the end of the Haka was deafening.

Ka mate, ka mate!	*It is death! It is death!*
Ka ora, ka ora!	*It is life! It is life!*
Ka mate! Ka mate!	*We're going to die!* *We're going to die!*
Ka ora! Ka ora!	*We're going to live!* *We're going to live!*
Tēnei te tangata pūhuruhuru	*This is the hairy man*
Nāna nei i tiki mai whakawhiti te rā.	*Who fetched the sun and made it shine.*
Ā upane! Ka upane!	*One step upward!* *Another step upward!*
Ā upane, ka upane – whiti te ra!	*An upward step, another upward step – the sun shines!*

Auckland kicked off, a high ball that fell to Rory, who made a perfect catch, then passed it ten metres across to Woody.

Woody charged. This was his first time going at the Auckland defence and Owen knew he would want to let their opponents know he was there. Two Auckland forwards came in at him hard. They seemed to know he was the man to stop. And they did stop him. But not until he'd gained eight metres.

Woody turned and set the ball down for Owen.

Owen picked the ball up and played it low to Sunil. Four phases later, Borderlands were ten metres out. Owen was thrilled. He loved the fast tempo Borderlands had begun with. They hadn't given the home team a minute to settle. He'd planned to build up points slowly all game, earning penalties, relying on Rory's kicking. But the speed and energy with which

Borderlands were attacking was too exciting to hold back.

Owen took the ball from a driving maul and span it out to Woody, who had already gathered momentum from deep. The momentum was so great that he took his two forwards with him. And now he had Andrew and Gareth behind him, pushing their shoulders at him, another driving maul, soon joined by David and Duncan. All the weight of the Borderlands pack focused behind Woody.

The force of it was irresistible.

Woody was over, his hands reaching down, placing the ball over the line.

A try.

Owen punched the air. It was hard to believe Borderlands had scored so quickly. 5–0 within three minutes. Then 7–0 after Rory's conversion. A fantastic way to show Auckland that they could compete.

But Owen knew he had to focus his troops. They had to keep their heads. They'd not faced the Auckland attack yet. And the thought of that made him very wary indeed.

Auckland kicked off again. Rhys took the ball this time, just before the Auckland forwards took him down. Owen was behind Sunil and ready to get the ball to the other backs. But this time his pass fell short.

His mistake.

And he knew it.

Borderlands had lost possession.

Now they were under pressure on their 22. Now they would see what the Auckland attack was like.

Right away Auckland exerted intense pressure. It was so intense that Owen could tell that all the Borderlands boys were struggling. He cursed himself. They were deep in their own half and deep in trouble, less than a minute after scoring the opening try.

With the ball for the first time, Auckland were ruthless. Their centres piled into Borderlands and cut through their defence. One pass, another pass, then a third, and they sliced through the Borderlands back line.

Try.

An all too easy try. An easy conversion, too.

7–7.

Then eight minutes later – after a handling error from Rhys after a scrum – another try. Not converted. 12–7 to Auckland.

This went on all first half. Borderlands would defend well enough and attack well enough too. But the attack always seemed to break down at a key moment. Owen knew why it was happening. Those key moments were

the kind of moments where Jesse would have sent out a killer pass.

Then, when Borderlands were on the back foot, they would crumble. The Auckland team would make ten or more metres and Owen would see panic on the faces of his team-mates. His own idea of a game based on building up penalty kicks was impossible to deliver in this frenzy of attack.

By half-time it was 29–7. Five tries against. Two converted.

As he led his players off at half-time, Owen stared at the ground. He'd never felt so dejected or defeated. What was he going to say now?

He was meant to be the captain. The leader.

How could he bring his team round from this, so that they could turn it round in the second half? How could he bring his team round from the stark truth that without Jesse as scrum half and captain, Borderlands were clumsy, error-prone and facing a severe thrashing?

THIRTEEN

Back under the huge main stand of Eden Park, Owen stood at the head of the tunnel and waited for his team-mates to leave the pitch for half-time. He patted each one of them on the back and said "Well tried" to them all.

They had tried hard.

Very hard.

Even so, they'd been utterly out-classed by Auckland Grammar School. 29–7 said it all.

As he came off, Owen looked up at the main stand and tried to think of the words he could say to his team-mates. What was a captain meant to say at half-time when the opposition had as good as won the game? Should he fire them up to try and make an astonishing comeback? Or should he suggest they just play for self-respect and avoid a cricket score?

This was a nightmare. Why had he let them choose him as captain?

He felt hopeless. Helpless. Horrible.

As he gazed into space, punishing himself, Owen saw a line of men and women file into two rows of seats not far from the front of the main stand. They were all dressed in blue. He looked again. RAF blue. Then he saw one of them waving to him, then three more. Then the whole group was waving at him.

Owen waved back and laughed. He could see Rory's mum and dad. And Woody's dad. Plus several other adults that he knew were the parents of some of his team-mates. As he waved at them, he saw what had happened. The RAF had flown the parents out to New Zealand. They'd come to Eden Park directly from the Central Asian Republic. They'd missed the first half, but they were here now.

That was why Woody and Rory had been unable to contact their parents.

Now Owen knew what he had to say.

He marched under the stand to his dressing room and asked Mr Johnson to step outside.

"I need a word, sir," Owen said.

"Owen, don't worry," Mr Johnson told him. "Auckland are a superb outfit. You're not to blame ..."

Owen shook his head. "No, sir. This is more important."

Mr Johnson looked puzzled. "What is it?"

"The parents. They're here."

"Fantastic," Mr Johnson said. "I didn't think they'd make it."

"You knew?" Owen said.

"I knew there was a plan."

"But you didn't want to disappoint the lads?"

"That's right. In case they didn't get here on time."

"So shall I tell them?" Owen asked. "It might affect the second half."

Mr Johnson nodded. "It will affect the second half, Owen. But this is your call, son. You're captain. What's your gut feeling?"

Owen thought about it for a moment. What was best for the boys whose mums and dads were out there, back from war? And what was best for the rest of the team? For their hopes of turning the game round?

Mr Johnson was waiting for an answer. Owen had a clear idea of what it was.

"We take the team out now," he said. "Spend five minutes talking to the parents in their stand. Then five minutes refocusing for the second half."

Mr Johnson smiled. "That's a fine idea, Owen. Go in there and tell them. Lead them out."

Owen went into the dressing room and asked his players to come back out onto the pitch.

"Why?" Gareth asked. "We need to regroup. Not spend more time out there."

"Trust me," Owen said. "Come on."

There were mutterings behind Owen as they walked back out along the tunnel and onto Eden Park. Once they were on the pitch, Owen turned the team round and pointed at the two rows of RAF personnel. Their faces were a picture.

"You've got five minutes to talk to your parents," Owen said. "No more. And don't go into the stands. Stay out here. Then I want you back on the pitch. I need you focused. We've a second half to play."

Owen knew he would never understand what it meant to have a parent away at war and in danger. He'd never understand what it was like not knowing when – or if – they were coming home.

But as he watched his team-mates reach out to their mums and dads, and the parents jump down to grab their kids, he had a decent idea.

The other fans in the stadium fell quiet so that the Borderlands boys could talk to their parents. They seemed to know what was going on.

Owen smiled and folded his arms.

No matter the score right now, it felt good to be a captain.

FOURTEEN

The second half was different to the first. Borderlands had a renewed spirit and a flow to their game. It paid off within five minutes.

Owen took the ball from the back of the scrum 25 metres out and fed it to Woody. Woody didn't battering-ram the Auckland defence – instead he played a long pass out to George on the wing, and took the Auckland back line by surprise. Thomas charged over, managing to keep his feet just inside the line.

Try. Converted by Rory.

29–14.

Now the gap between the teams didn't look so wide.

The game didn't feel like such a lost cause.

But it did when Auckland broke through on 49 minutes. And again on 67 minutes. One try converted. One missed.

In between Woody had scored a single try. And Rory had missed the conversion.

With only four minutes left, Owen eyed the scoreboard. 41–19.

The game was lost and it had been lost by the end of the first half. He knew it. Everyone knew it. Borderlands would not be world champions.

But Owen knew there was one thing that would make his team feel less bad about defeat. They could still win the second half. It was a target, a focus. That would make a difference to the team. And to the parents who had missed the first half anyway. If Borderlands could score once, then the parents would have seen

Borderlands score more points than Auckland. That would feel like a victory of sorts.

Owen had seen the parents amassing near the tunnel area, ready to run onto the pitch as soon as the whistle blew for the end of the game. They couldn't wait to get hold of their sons.

One score would do it. A penalty. A try. Or a drop goal. One score that would make the parents – and their sons – happy.

So, during a break in play – when Auckland were bringing on a sub – Owen spoke to Woody and Rory. He could tell his friends were shattered and keen for the game to end, so they could see their parents.

"We can win this half," Owen said.

"OK," both his friends said. They were breathing deeply, hands on hips.

"The three of us need to set it up," Owen said. "I'll feed you, Woody, off this scrum.

We're 40 metres out. Woody, make as much ground as you can. I'll be behind you. Push the ball back to me, then Rory, you stay centre of the field, ready for a pass. Then drop it. OK?"

"OK," both his friends said again.

Then Owen wound his pack up, shouting at them to win the scrum, to win it for the parents.

Borderlands took the Auckland pack by surprise with their power – and they won it easily.

Owen waited until he could see Woody charging towards him, then he tossed the ball crisply into his path.

Woody was running at pace, but he was brought down having made five metres. It was a great effort. Owen reached for the ball, hesitated and saw that Rory was in place. Forty metres out. A long way for an under-15 to score a drop goal.

But Owen had faith.

He plucked the ball from the ground and span it out to Rory.

Rory took it cleanly, dropped the ball and fired it high towards the far stand of Eden Park. It sailed in between the posts. Perfect.

41–22.

Anyone coming into Eden Park at the end of the game, who saw 20 or so adults run onto the pitch and grab their sons, would think that the team in yellow and blue had just won the World Cup. If they'd looked at the faces of the Borderlands team, they'd have thought the same. Huge grins. Tears. Hugs. Arms draped round each other.

They would have also thought that Auckland Grammar School were the losers, the way they stood and applauded Borderlands, paying respect to the team and their parents.

But the truth was something completely different.

Owen watched Woody's dad sprinting across the grass to grab his son. And Rory going the other way to leap at both of his parents.

He knew how intense the emotions were that his friends would be feeling now. He'd been with them every day for the months that they'd had to be apart from their parents. He'd talked to them, given them space and tried, at times, to use rugby to distract them.

Owen didn't need to do that now.

Borderlands had lost the final of the World Schools Rugby Trophy.

But it didn't matter.

They had just won so much more.

FIFTEEN

After Borderlands had stood and clapped the Auckland team as they went up to receive the trophy, Owen jogged over to Kane. "Storming," he said. "Congratulations."

"Cheers, mate. That was a blinding second half."

"Thanks," Owen said with a grin. "How about we swap shirts?"

Kane nodded. "Love to."

The two boys swapped shirts, shook hands, then Owen watched Kane go off to celebrate with his team-mates.

He felt proud to have played against Auckland – and to have Kane's shirt. He felt elated like never before. He was looking forward.

To next season.

To playing more rugby.

And to tonight – after the post-match party – when he would read the last few pages of *Calon*. He would finish it and then think which book he would like to read next.

ACKNOWLEDGEMENTS

Thanks are due to my wife, my daughter and my agent, David Luxton; to my writing group, Ali Taft, Anna Turner and James Nash. To the children and teachers at Albrighton Primary School, led by the aptly named Mr Auckland, and the men and women of RAF Cosford. To Theo and Steven Price for being this book's first readers. And to Barrington Stoke. Thank you!

This book was written with the generous support of Arts Council England and the Society of Authors, who helped fund a research trip to New Zealand. In New Zealand, I was given superb assistance by the wonderful people at Eden Park and by Grant Hansen at Auckland Grammar School. Alison Hewitt at Kristin School gave me excellent advice. I am indebted to them all.

Our books are tested
for children and young people by
children and young people.

Thanks to everyone who consulted on
a manuscript for their time and effort in
helping us to make our books better
for our readers.